ב"ה

Sara Finds a Mitzva

I dedicate this book to my amazing children, Avigail, Mordecai, and Chana, who constantly remind me about the importance of doing a mitzva. R.S.

In memory of "Daddy Fix-It," Walter J. Herbst. M.W.

First Edition – 2010 / 5770
PJ Library Edition – 2023 / 5783
Copyright © 2010 by HACHAI PUBLISHING
Artwork © 2010 copyright by Michael Weber
ALL RIGHTS RESERVED

Editor: D.L. Rosenfeld
Managing Editor: Yossi Leverton
Layout: Moshe Cohen

ISBN: 978-1-929628-46-9
(Hardcover edition)
LCCN: 2009942798
0723/B0717/A4

Printed in China.

GLOSSARY	
Bubby	Yiddish word for grandmother
Hashavas Aveida	The mitzva of returning lost items
Kosher	"Fit," prepared according to Jewish dietary laws
Mitzva	One of the 613 commandments; good deed

Sara Finds a Mitzva

by **Rebeka Simhaee**
illustrated by **Michael Weber**

One warm and sunny morning, Sara skipped along next to her bubby. They were on their way to mail a letter at the corner mailbox.

Sara liked it when she could put in the letter by herself.
She reached up, standing on tiptoe, when suddenly she
noticed something.

Right on top of the mailbox sat a little toy duck.
It had shiny black button eyes and soft white wings.

"Look what I found," said Sara.
The little duck fit just perfectly in her arms.

Bubby looked at Sara and said gently, "I think there's a very sad little boy or girl missing that toy, don't you?"

Sara thought about that for a moment. "There must be," she said slowly. "Let's try to find out so we can give it back."

"That would be a mitzva," said Bubby.
"Do you know which one?"

Sara nodded. "Hashavas Aveida!"

"That's right," said Bubby,
"the mitzva of returning lost things."

"But where do we start?" asked Sara. "I don't
see any sad little boys or girls around here!"

"Look, here's a clue," said Bubby. She pointed to a candy wrapper stuck to the mailbox. "This wrapper is from Gold's Candy Store. Let's go and see if anyone there knows who owns this toy."

So Bubby and Sara walked across the street to the candy store.

"Hello," said Mr. Gold.

"Hi," said Sara. "Bubby and I found this cute toy duck. Do you know who lost it?"

"Well," answered the storekeeper, "I remember seeing it when a little girl came into my store with her mother. But I don't know her name or where she lives."

"Oh, no," said Sara. "Now what should we do?"

"You know," said Mr. Gold, "they did throw something in the wastebasket before they left."

"It's a clue," said Bubby.
She picked up a crumpled
piece of paper.

"This has the address of Shula's Dress Shop.
Maybe someone there can help us."

Together, Bubby and Sara hurried out of the store.
Sara didn't even ask Bubby to buy any candy.

She just couldn't wait to find that girl!

At the dress shop, Sara asked Shula, "Has a little girl been to your store? She lost her duck, and we want to return it to her."

Shula smiled. "Yes, a little girl was just here, but I don't know where she went next."

"That's okay," said Sara. "Maybe we can find another clue."

Everyone looked around. On the floor, right under a rack of fancy dresses, lay a colorful birthday hat.

Sara ran and picked it up.

"Do you think today could be that girl's birthday? Maybe she and her mother walked to the bakery to buy a birthday cake!"

"Let's go see," answered Bubby. And off they went.

At Aaron's Kosher Bakery, Sara asked, "Excuse me, did a little girl come in with her mother to buy a birthday cake?"

Bubby explained, "That girl lost her toy duck, and we'd like to return it to her."

"Oh," Aaron replied, "what a nice mitzva! I did sell a birthday cake to a little girl and her mother, but how can you figure out where they are now?"

Sara sighed. "We need another clue."

Together, they looked around the bakery.
There was nothing on the floor or in the wastebasket.

There were no clues at all.

Suddenly, Sara pointed to a poster on the wall.
"What does it say, Bubby?"

"It's a sign about a sale at the toy store."

Sara got excited.

"I think they went to buy a birthday present at the toy store. Oh, Bubby, let's go find her!"

Bubby opened the door to the toy store, and Sara rushed in.

Usually she loved to stop and look at all the toys and dolls and prizes, but not today.

"Don't worry, little duck," said Sara. "We are going to find your owner. Yes, we are!"

"Oh, my!" Bubby laughed. "There are so many little girls here with their mothers. How will we ever find the right one?"

"I know!" said Sara.
She walked right up to one of the girls and asked,
"Did you lose something today?"

The girl's eyes grew wide. "I did lose something...
a little toy duck! Thank you for giving it back.

"But, how did you know it was mine?"

Sara pointed to a shopping bag full of candy, a pretty dress covered in plastic, colorful party hats, and a big cake box.

"Look," she said. "Look at all these clues! They helped me find my mitzva."

As they made their way home, Sara felt the happiness of her mitzva bubbling up inside her.

But her arms seemed empty without that duck to carry.

Bubby noticed and smiled at her granddaughter.

"A girl who tried so hard to find a mitzva deserves a little gift, don't you think?"

Then Bubby pulled something
out of her bag especially for Sara.

It was her very own duck with shiny black button eyes
and soft white wings!